Baby Loves

Michael Lawrence

Illustrated by Adrian Reynolds

DK PUBLISHING, INC.

www.dk.com

Baby loves

Mommy and

Daddy more than anything in the world. Except...

Breakfast

Baby loves breakfast
more than anything
in the world except...

Teddy

Baby loves Teddy more than anything in the world except...

Kitty

Baby loves Kitty more than anything in the world except...

Slippers

Baby loves slippers more than anything in the world except...

Flowers

Baby loves flowers
more than anything
in the world except...

Granny

Baby loves Granny more than anything in the world except...

Hat

Baby loves hat
more than
anything in
the world
except...

Baby loves sunshine more than anything in the world except...

Rain

Baby loves rain more than anything in the world except...

Drum

Baby loves drum more than
anything in the world except....

Duckie

Baby loves Duckie more than

anything in the world except...

Bathtime

Baby loves bathtime more than anything in the world except...

Bedtime

And Mommy and Daddy
love Baby more
than anything
in the world except...

No.

Mommy and

Daddy love

Baby

more than anything

in the world...

Anything at all!

For Jemima and Max Gee, proud new parents — M.L.
For Julian, Isabel, and Joseph — A.R.

A DK PUBLISHING BOOK
www.dk.com

First American Edition, 1999
4 6 8 10 9 7 5 3

Published in the United States by DK Publishing, Inc.
95 Madison Avenue, New York, New York 10016

Printed in Hong Kong by Wing King Tong

Library of Congress Cataloging-in-Publication Data
Lawrence, Michael (Michael C.)
Baby loves / written by Michael Lawrence; illustrated
by Adrian Reynolds — 1st ed.   p.   cm.
Summary: Baby's attention is fickle to all the wonderful things he
encounters through the day, but his parents' love for him is constant.
ISBN 0-7894-3410-5 (Hardback)
ISBN 0-7894-4596-4 (Paperback)
(1. Babies — Fiction. 2. Day — Fiction. 3. Parent and child — Fiction.)
I. Reynolds, Adrian, ill. II. Title.
PZ7.L4368Bab   1998
[E] — dc21   97-45858
                                              CIP
                                              AC